The Mexican Twins

Lucy Fitch Perkins

The Mexican Twins

I

SAN RAMON'S DAY IN THE MORNING

I

ONE summer morning the red rooster on his perch in the fig tree woke up and took a look at the sky.

He was a very responsible rooster. He was always the first one up in the morning, and I really think he believed that if it were not for him the sun himself would forget to rise.

It was so very early that a few stars still shone, and a pale moon was sailing away toward the west. Over the eastern hills the rooster saw a pink cloud, and knew at once that it was time to wake the world. He stood up and stretched his wings. Then he crowed so long and loud that he nearly fell off his perch backward, on to the cat, who was sleeping on the roof just below.

"Cock a doodle do-o-o!" he screamed. "I'm awake, are you-oo-oo?"

At least that is the way it must have sounded to all the other roosters in the little village, for they began at once to answer him.

"Cock a doodle doo-oo, we're up as soon as you-oo," they cried; and soon there was such a chorus of them calling back and forth that the five hens woke up, one after another, and flew down from the perch, to hunt bugs for their breakfast.

Last of all the turkey opened his eyes and flapped heavily to the ground, gobbling all the way.

The cat stretched herself and sprang from the roof to the fig tree and sharpened her claws on its bark.

The birds began to sing, and still there was no sound from the tiny gray adobe house under the fig tree.

The little white hen tiptoed round to the front of the hut and peeped in at the open door. There in one corner of their one room lay Tonio and Tita and their father and mother, all sound asleep.

The little white hen must have told the red rooster what she saw, for he followed her and looked into the hut too. Then he ruffled his neck feathers, flapped his wings, and crowed so loudly that Pancho and Doña Teresa and the Twins all woke at once and sat up with a bounce, to see what was the matter.

It startled the little white hen to see them all sit up suddenly in a row, so she squawked and scrambled out through the open door as fast as she could go.

The red rooster ran too, and the two of them never stopped until they disappeared behind the bee-hives in the garden.

II

The moment she was really awake, Doña Teresa began to talk.

"Upon my soul!" she cried, crossing herself, "the red rooster gave me a dreadful turn. I was just in the midst of a most beautiful dream! But now he has driven it all out of my head with his silly noise, and I cannot even remember what it was about!"

Doña Teresa rose, and while she talked she deftly rolled up the mat on which she had slept and stood it on end in the corner of the room. You see it didn't take any time at all to dress, because they always slept with their clothes on. But Doña Teresa was very particular about one thing. She made them all wash their faces and hands the very first thing every single morning!

For a wash-basin there was a part of a log, hollowed out like a trough. Beside the hollow log there was a large red olla, with a gourd in it. Pancho had dipped water from the olla into the trough and was already splashing about, while Doña Teresa rolled the Twins off on to the floor and placed their mats in the corner with the others.

"Come, my pigeons," she said to them, "it is time to be stirring. We are very lazy to lie in bed after cockcrow on San Ramon's Day!"

"Oh, Little Mother," cried Tita, picking herself up, "is it really the fiesta of San Ramon? And may I take the little white hen to be blessed, all myself?"

"You may take the little white hen if you can catch her," Doña Teresa answered. "Indeed, we must take all the animals, or at the very least one of each kind to stand for all the others. The turkey must be caught, and the goat must be brought from the field so I can milk her. Tonto [that was what they called the donkey] is waiting in the shed to be made ready, not to speak of the cat and dog! Bless my soul, how many things there are to be done!"

While his mother talked, Tonio had taken his lasso down from the nail where it hung, and was just quietly slipping out of the door with it, when Doña Teresa saw him. "Here you — Tonio," she cried, "come back and wash yourself!"

"Can't I wait until I've caught Pinto?" Tonio begged. "What's the use of washing? You only get dirty again. Lots of the boys don't wash at all except on Sunday."

"Come right back and wash yourself this minute," commanded Doña Teresa. "You might as well say it's no use to eat your breakfast because you'll be hungry again right away! As long as I'm your mother you shall begin the day right at least."

Tonio groaned a little, and came back to the trough. There he did something that he called washing, though I feel quite sure that there were corners behind his ears that were not even wet!

On the wall above the place where the sleeping mats had been spread, there was a picture of the Virgin and Child, and Doña Teresa kept a little taper always burning before the picture.

When they had all washed, Doña Teresa called Pancho and the Twins to her side, and all four knelt in a row before the picture, crossed themselves, and murmured a little prayer.

"If you want the day to go right," said Doña Teresa as she rose from her knees, "always begin with saying your prayers and washing your face. And now, Tonio, run and catch Pinto for your father while I get his breakfast, for the cows must be rounded up for milking even if it is San Ramon's Day; and Tita, you take the little red olla and go for water!"

III

While the Twins were gone on these errands, Pancho fed the donkey, and Doña Teresa made the fire in her queer little stove; only she didn't call it a stove—she called it a brasero. It was a sort of box built up of clay and stones. The brasero stood in an alcove, and beside it was a large red olla, which Doña Teresa kept filled with water for her cooking. Beyond the brasero was a cupboard for the dishes.

Doña Teresa knelt before the brasero and pulled out the ashes of yesterday's fire. Then she put in some little sticks, lighted them, and set a flat red dish on top of the brasero over the tiny flames.

In the corner of the room there was a pretty basket covered with a white drawn-work napkin. Doña Teresa turned back the napkin and counted out ten flat cakes, made of corn meal. They were yesterday's tortillas. These she put in the dish to heat.

When they were warm, she brought some of them to Pancho, with a dish of beans and red chile sauce. Pancho sat down on a flat stone under the fig tree to eat his breakfast. He had no knife or fork or spoon, but he really did not need them, for he tore the tortillas into wedge-shaped pieces and scooped up the beans and chile sauce with them, and ate scoop, beans, chile sauce, and all in one mouthful. The chile sauce was so hot with red pepper that you would have thought that Pancho must have had a tin throat in order to swallow it at all; but he was used to it, and never even winked his eyes when it went down. Just as he was taking the last bite of the last tortilla, Tonio came back, leading Pinto by the rope of his lasso.

Tonio was very proud of catching Pinto and bringing him back to his father all by himself. He even put the saddle on. But the moment he felt the saddle-girth around him Pinto swelled up like everything, so that Tonio couldn't buckle it! Tonio pulled and tugged until he was red in the face, but Pinto just stood still with his ears turned back, and stayed swelled.

Then Pancho came up. He took hold of the strap, braced his knee against Pinto's side, and pulled.

6

Pinto knew it was no use holding his breath any longer, so he let go, and in a minute Pancho had the strap securely fastened and had vaulted into the saddle.

He was just starting away, when Doña Teresa came running out of the hut with something in her hand. "Here's a bite of lunch for you," she said, "in case you get hungry in the field. There's beans and chile sauce and four tortillas."

She had put it all nicely in a little dish with the tortillas fitted in like a cover over the chile sauce and beans, and it was all tied up in a clean white cloth.

Pancho took off his sombrero, put the dish carefully on his head, and clapped his hat down over it. The hat was large, and the dish just fitted the crown, so it seemed quite safe. Then he galloped off, looking very grand and gay, with his red serape flying out behind him.

When he was out of sight, Doña Teresa and the Twins had their breakfasts too, sitting on the stones under the fig tree.

II

THE BLESSING

I

WHEN breakfast was over you could tell by the long, long shadow of the fig tree that it was still very early in the morning. On sunny days Doña Teresa could tell the time almost exactly by its shadow, but on rainy days she just had to guess, because there was no clock in her little cabin.

It was lucky that it was so early, because there were so many things to be done. The Twins and their mother were not the only busy people about, however, for there were two hundred other peons beside Pancho who worked on the hacienda, and each one had a little cabin where he lived with his family.

There were other vaqueros besides Pancho. There were ploughmen, and farmers, and water-carriers, and servants for the great white house where Señor Fernandez lived with his wife and pretty daughter Carmen. And there was the gatekeeper, José, whom the Twins loved because he knew the most wonderful stories and was always willing to tell them.

There were field-workers, and wood-cutters, and even fishermen. The huts where they all lived were huddled together like a little village, and the village, and the country for miles and miles around, and the big house, and the little chapel beside it, and the schoolhouse, and everything else on that great hacienda, belonged to Señor Fernandez.

It almost seemed as if the workers all belonged to Señor Fernandez, too, for they had to do just what he told them to, and there was no other place for them to go and nothing else for them to do if they had wanted ever so much to change.

All the people, big and little, loved the fiesta of San Ramon. They thought the priest's blessing would cause the hens to lay more eggs, and the cows to give more milk, and that it would keep all the creatures well and strong.

Though it was a feast day, most of the men had gone away from their homes early, when Pancho did; but the women and children in all the little cabins were busy as bees, getting themselves and their animals ready to go in procession to the place where the priest was to bless them.

As soon as breakfast was eaten, Doña Teresa said to Tonio: "Go now, my Tonio, and make Tonto beautiful! His coat is rough and full of burs, and he will make a very poor figure to show the priest unless you give him a good brushing. Only be careful of his hind legs. You know Tonto is sometimes very wild with his hind legs. It is strange to me that his front ones should be so much more tame, but it seems to be the nature of the poor creature."

Tonio went to Tonto's shed and brought him out and tied him to a tree. Then he brushed his coat and took out the burs, and braided the end of his tail, and even made a wreath of green leaves and hung it over his left ear. And Tonto seemed to know that it was San Ramon's Day, for he never kicked at all, and brayed only once, when Tonio pulled a very large bur out of his ear.

II

While Tonio was making Tonto beautiful, Tita swept the ground under the fig tree and sprinkled it with water, and washed and put away the few dishes they had used.

Her mother was very busy meanwhile, grinding the corn for tortillas. You see, every single meal they had tortillas. It was their bread, and their meat too, most of the time, so it would never do to miss getting the corn ground, not even if it were the greatest feast day of the whole year.

When Tita had finished putting things in order, her mother said to her, "Now, my pigeon, see if you can't catch the little white hen, and the red rooster, and the turkey. The red rooster crows so sweetly I shall miss him when he is put in the pot, but he is not long for this world! He is so greedy there's no satisfying him with food. He has no usefulness at all, except to wake us in the morning.

"But the little white hen now! There is the useful one! She has already begun to lay. She must surely go to the priest. And as for the turkey, he needs to go for the sake of his temper! I hope the padrecito will lay a spell

9

on him to stop his gobbling from morning till night. It will be no grief to me when he is put on to boil."

The red rooster, the hen, and the turkey were all wandering round in the little patch of garden behind the house, when Tita came out, rattling some corn in a dish.

The red rooster began to run the moment he heard corn rattle, and he called to the hens to come too. He seemed to think they wouldn't know enough even to eat corn unless he advised them to.

They swarmed around Tita's feet, pecking at each other and snatching greedily at each kernel as it fell.

"You all need to go to the priest for your manners," Tita said to them severely. "You behave like the pigs."

She set the dish down on the ground, and when they all tried to get their heads into it at once, she picked out the legs of the red rooster and seized them with one hand, and those of the little white hen with the other, and before they could guess what in the world was happening to them she had them safely in the house, where she tied them to the legs of the table.

III

When Tita went back after the turkey, she found him eating the very last kernels of corn out of the dish. He had driven all the hens away and was having a very nice time by himself. Tita made a grab for his legs, but he was too quick for her. He flew up into the fig tree and from there to the roof. Tita looked up at him anxiously.

"Don't you think you ought to get blessed?" she said. "Come down now, that's a good old gobbler! Mother says your temper is so bad you must surely go to the priest, and how can I take you if you won't come down?"

"Gobble," said the turkey, and stayed where he was.

Tita was in despair. She threw a stick at him, but he only walked up the thatched roof with his toes turned in, and sat down on the ridge-pole.

Just then Tita looked down the river path, and there was Tonio coming with the goat! At least he was trying to, but the goat didn't seem to care any more about being blessed than the turkey did. She was standing with her four feet braced, pulling back with all her might, while Tonio pulled forward on the lasso which was looped over her horns.

Tonio looked very angry. He called to Tita, "Come here and help me with this fool of a goat! I believe the devil himself has got into her! She has acted just like this all the way from the pasture!"

Tita ran down the path and got behind the goat. She pushed and Tonio pulled, and by and by they got her as far as the fig tree. Then they tied her to a branch, and while Doña Teresa milked her, the Twins went after the turkey again.

Tonio had practiced lassoing bushes and stumps and pigs and chickens and even Tita herself, ever since he could remember, and you may be sure no turkey could get the best of him. He stood down in the yard and whirled his lasso in great circles round his head, and then all of a sudden the loop flew into the air and dropped right over the turkey on the ridge-pole, and tightened around his legs!

If he hadn't had wings the turkey certainly would have tumbled off the roof. As it was, he spread his wings and flopped down, and Tita took him into the cabin and tied him to the third leg of the table. There he made himself very disagreeable to the little white hen, and gobbled angrily at the red rooster, and even pecked at Tita herself when she came near.

"There!" sighed Doña Teresa, when the turkey was safely tied; "at last we have them all together. Now we will make them all gay."

She went to the chest which held all their precious things, took out three rolls of tissue paper, and held them up for the Twins to see. One was green, one was white, and one was red.

"Look," said she. "These are all Mexican animals, so I thought it would be nice for them to wear the Mexican colors. Come, my angels, and I will show you how to make wreaths and streamers and fringes and flowers for them to wear. Our creatures must not shame us by looking shabby and dull in the procession. They shall be as gay as the best of them."

For a long time they all three worked, and when they had made enough decorations for all the animals, Doña Teresa brought out another surprise. It was some gilt paint and a brush! She let Tonio gild the goat's horns and hoofs, and Tita gilded the legs and feet of the little white hen.

While she was doing it, the red rooster stuck his bill into the dish and swallowed two great big bites of gold paint on his own account! Doña Teresa saw him do it.

"If he isn't trying to gild himself on the inside!" she cried. "Did you ever see such sinful pride!" And then she made him swallow a large piece of red pepper because she was afraid the paint would disagree with him.

The red rooster seemed depressed for a long time after that; but whether it was because of the paint, or the pepper, or being so awfully dressed up, I cannot say. His bill was gilded because he had dipped it in the gold paint, so they gilded his legs to match. Then they tied a white tissue-paper wreath with long streamers around his neck. They tied a red one on the little white hen. They tried to decorate the turkey, too, but he was in no mood for it, and gobbled and pecked at them so savagely that Doña Teresa had to tie up his head in a rag!

They stuck some red tissue-paper flowers in Tonto's wreath, and tied red tissue-paper streamers to the goat's horns. They put a green ruff around the cat's neck, and a red one on the dog; but the dog ran at once to the river and waded in and got it all wet, and the color ran out and dyed his coat, and the ruff fell off, before they were even ready to start.

IV

At last a gong sounded from the big house.

The gong was the signal for the procession to start, and the moment they heard it, the people began pouring out of their cabins, and getting their animals together to drive toward the place where the blessing was to be.

Doña Teresa and Tita threw their rebozos over their heads, and Tonio put on his sombrero. Then Doña Teresa untied the turkey's legs and took him in her arms; and though his head was still tied in the cloth, he gobbled like everything.

Tita took the little white hen on one arm, and her kitten on the other, and Tonio led the donkey, with Jasmin following behind.

They were all ready to start, when Doña Teresa cried out, "Upon my soul! We nearly forgot the goat! Surely she's needing a blessing as much as the worst of them."

She hurried back to the fig tree and untied the goat with one hand, because she was still carrying the turkey with the other. When the goat felt herself free, she gave a great jump and nearly jerked the rope out of Doña Teresa's hand; then she went galloping toward the gate so fast that poor Doña Teresa was all out of breath keeping up with her.

"Bless my soul, but that goat goes gayly!" she panted, as she joined the Twins at the gate. "If I led her about much I should have no chance to get fat."

Already there were crowds of people and animals going by. It was a wonderful procession. There were horses and cows all gayly decorated with garlands and colored streamers. There were donkeys and pigs and guinea-fowls and cats and dogs and birds in cages, and so many other creatures that it looked very much like the procession of animals going into Noah's ark.

Doña Josefa, who lived in a hut near the river, was driving two ducks and two white geese,—only she had dyed the geese a bright purple,—and José's wife had painted stripes of red clear around her pig. She was having a dreadful time keeping the pig in the road, for all the little boys, and all the little dogs—and there were a great many of both—frisked and gamboled around the procession and got in the way, and made such a noise that it is no wonder the creatures were distracted and tried to run away.

V

It was not a very great distance to the large corrals back of the big house where the people were to meet, and as they drew near the grounds Tonio and Tita could see Pancho dashing about on Pinto after stray cows, and other cowboys rounding up the calves and putting them in a corral by themselves.

The bulls were already safely shut away in another inclosure, and all the open space around the corrals was filled with horses, and donkeys, and sheep, and goats, and dogs, and cats, and fowls of all kinds, all dressed in such gay colors and making such a medley of sounds that the Fourth of July, fire-crackers and all, would have seemed like Sunday afternoon beside the celebration of San Ramon's Day in Mexico.

Señor Fernandez, looking very grand in his black velvet suit and big sombrero, sat on his fine horse and watched the scene. Beside him, on their own horses, were Doña Paula, his wife, and pretty Carmen, their daughter.

The servants of the big house were grouped around them, and all the rest of the people passed back and forth among the animals, trying to make them keep still and behave themselves until the priest should appear.

It was not long before the priest came out of his house, with a small boy beside him carrying a basin of holy water.

Doña Teresa and all the people knelt on the ground when they saw him coming. The priest walked among them chanting a prayer and sprinkling drops of holy water over the animals and over the people too. Of course the people behaved very well, but I am sorry to have to tell you that when he felt the drops of water fall on the rag that his head was tied up in, the turkey gobbled just exactly as if it were Tita—or Doña Teresa—instead of the priest!

And the cat stuck up her tail and arched her back, in a most impolite way. Perhaps that was not to be wondered at, because we all know that cats can never bear water, not even holy water.

But when Tonto, who should have known better, and who was used to being out in the rain even, stuck his nose up in the air and let out a "hee-haw, hee-haw" that set every other donkey in the crowd hee-hawing too, Doña Teresa felt as if she should die of mortification.

Only the red rooster, the little white hen, the goat, and the Twins behaved as if they had had any bringing up at all! However, the priest didn't seem to mind it. He went in and out among the people, sprinkling the water and chanting his prayer until the basin was empty. Then he pronounced the blessing.

VI

When he had finished, the people drove their creatures back to their homes, or to the fields.

Pancho came riding along and took Tita and the white hen up on Pinto's back with him. Tonio rode Tonto and carried the rooster. Tita had to put the cat down to get up on the horse, and when Tonio's dog saw her he barked at her, and she ran just as fast as she could and got to the cabin and up on the roof out of reach.

Doña Teresa walked along with Doña Josefa, and talked with her about her rheumatism and about how badly the animals behaved, and how handsome Doña Josefa's purple geese were, until she turned in at their own gate.

When she was in their own yard once more, she set the turkey down and untied his head. Tonio let the rooster go, and Tita set the little white hen free, and they all three ran under Tonto's shed as if they were afraid they might get blessed again if they stayed where they could easily be caught. And they never came out until they had torn the tissue paper all to pieces and left it lying on the ground.

Tonio got the goat back to pasture by walking in front of her, holding a carrot just out of reach, and Pancho took Pinto and the donkey down to the river for a drink, while Tita and her mother went into the cabin to get the second breakfast ready. When people get up so very early they need two breakfasts.

Doña Teresa was just patting the meal into cakes with her hands and cooking them over the brasero, when Pancho came in the cabin door with dreadful red streams running down his head and face and over his white cotton clothes!

15

When Doña Teresa saw him, she screamed and flew to his side. "What is it, my Pancho?" she cried. "You are hurt—you are killed, my angel! Oh, what has happened?"

She asked so many questions and poured out so many words that Pancho couldn't get one in edgewise; so he just took off his hat, and there was the dish of chile sauce and tortillas broken all to bits, and the chile sauce spilled all over his face and clothes!

"It was that foolish Tonto that did it," he said, when he could say anything at all. "I was just putting him back in his shed when he cried, 'Hee-haw,' and let fly with both hind feet at once and one of them just grazed my head, and broke the dish."

Doña Teresa sat down heavily with her hand on her heart. "If anything had happened to you, my rose, my angel," she said, "I should have died of sorrow! Tonto is indeed a very careless beast. It would seem as if the padrecito's blessing might have put more sense into him. It must be the will of God that there should be a great deal of foolishness in the world, but without doubt donkeys and goats have more than their share."

Just then she smelled the tortillas burning and ran back to attend to them, while Pancho washed himself at the trough, and mopped the chile sauce off his clothes.

In a little while the Twins and their father and mother were all sitting about on the stones under the fig tree, eating their second breakfast. And when they had all had every bit they could hold, it was almost noon.

III

THE PARTY

I

EARLY that evening, when Pancho had rounded up the cows and taken them back again to pasture, and the goat had been milked, the animals fed, and supper eaten and cleared away, the Twins and their father and mother sat down together outside their cabin door.

The moon had risen and was shining so brightly that it made beautiful patterned shadows under the fig tree. There were pleasant evening sounds all about. Sometimes it was the hoot of an owl or the chirp of a cricket, but oftener it was the sound of laughter and of children's voices from the huts near by.

The red rooster, the turkey, and the hens were all asleep in the fig tree. Tita could see their bunchy shadows among the shadows of the leaves. The cat was away hunting for field-mice. Jasmin sat beside Tonio, with his tongue hanging out, and everything was very quiet and peaceful.

Then suddenly, quite far away, they heard a faint tinkling sound. "Ting-a-ling-ling; ting-a-ling-ling," it went, and then there was a voice singing:

The voice came nearer and nearer, and children's voices began to join in the singing, and soon Tonio and Tita could see dark forms moving in the moonlight. There was one tall figure, and swarming around it there were ever so many short ones.

"It's José with his guitar!" cried the Twins, and they flew out to meet him. Doña Teresa and Pancho came too.

"God give you good evening," they all cried out to each other when they met; and then José said, "Have you plenty of sweet potatoes, Doña Teresa? We have come with our dishes and our pennies."

"Yes," laughed Doña Teresa. "I thought you might come to-night and I knew your sweet tooth, José! And all these little ones, have they each got a sweet tooth too?"

"Oh yes, Doña Teresa, please cook us some sweet potatoes, won't you?" the children begged. They held up their empty dishes.

"Well, then, come in, all of you," said Doña Teresa, "and I will see what I can do."

She hurried back to the cabin. Pancho went with her, and José and the Twins and all the other children came trooping after them and swarmed around the cabin door.

Pancho made a little brasero right in the middle of the open space beside the fig tree. He made it of stones, and built a fire in it. While he was doing that, Doña Teresa got her sweet potatoes ready to cook, and when she came out with the cooking-dish and a jug of syrup in her hands, the children set up a shout of joy.

"Now sit down, all of you," commanded Doña Teresa, as she knelt beside the brasero and poured the syrup into the cooking-pan, "It will take some time to cook enough for every one, and if you are in too much of a hurry you may burn your fingers and your tongue. José, you tell us a story while we are waiting."

So they all sat down in a circle around Doña Teresa with José opposite her, and the fire flickered in the brasero, and lighted up all the eager brown faces and all the bright black eyes, as they watched Doña Teresa's cooking-pan.

II

Then José told the story of Br'er Rabbit and the Tar Baby; and after that he told how Br'er Rabbit made a riding-horse out of Br'er Fox; and when he had finished, the sweet potatoes were ready.

"Who shall have the first piece?" asked Doña Teresa, holding up a nice brown slice.

"José, José," cried all the children.

José took out his penny and gave it to Doña Teresa, and held out his dish. She took up a big piece of sweet potato on the end of a pointed stick. It was

18

almost safely landed in José's dish, when suddenly there was a great flapping of wings and a loud "Cock-a-doodle-doo," right behind José!

The red rooster had opened his eyes, and when he saw the glow of the fire, he thought it must be morning. So he crowed at once, and then flew right down off his perch, and before any one knew what he was after or could stop him, he had snatched José's candied sweet potato off the end of Doña Teresa's stick, and was running away with it as fast as he could go!

"Thanks be to God," said José, "that piece was still very hot!"

The red rooster soon found that out for himself. He was so afraid that somebody would get his morsel away from him that he swallowed it whole, boiling hot syrup and all! He thought it was worse than the red pepper and the gold paint he had taken that morning.

He opened his bill wide and squawked with pain, and his eyes looked wild. The children rolled on the ground with laughter. The last they saw of the red rooster he was running to the back of the house, where a dish of water was kept for the chickens; and it is perfectly true that for three days after that he could hardly crow at all!

Doña Teresa was dreadfully ashamed of the red rooster. She apologized and gave José another piece of sweet potato at once, and then she passed out more pieces to the children, and said: —

"Now mind you don't behave like the rooster! You see what he got for being greedy."

The children sucked their pieces slowly, so as to make them last a long time, and while they got themselves all sticky with syrup, José told them the story of Cinderella and her glass slippers and her pumpkin coach, and two ghost stories.

III

"Where did you learn so many beautiful stories, José?" asked Tonio when he had finished the last one. "Did you read them out of a book?" (You see Tonio and Tita and some of the older children went to school and were beginning to read a little.)

José shook his head. "No," he said, "I didn't read them out of books. I never had a chance to go to school when I was a boy. I tell you these stories just as they were told to me by my mother when I was as small as you are. And she couldn't read either, so somebody must have told them to her. Not everything comes from books, you see."

"Yes," said Doña Teresa. "I heard them from my mother when I was a child, and she couldn't read any more than Pancho and I can. But with these children here it will be different. They can get stories from you, and out of the books too. It is a great thing to have learning, though a peon can get along with very little of it, praise God."

Up to this time Pancho had not said a single word. He had brought sticks for the fire and had listened silently to the stories; but now he spoke.

"When the peons get enough learning, they will learn not to be peons at all," he said.

"But whatever will they be then?" gasped Doña Teresa. "Surely they must be whatever the good God made them, and if they are born peons—"

She stopped and looked a little alarmed, as if she thought perhaps after all it might be as well for Tonio and Tita to be like most of the people she knew—quite unable to read or write.

She crossed herself, and snatched Tita to her breast.

"You shall not learn enough to make you fly away from the nest, my bird!" she said.

Then Pancho spoke again. "With girls it does not matter," he said. "Girls do not need to know any thing but how to grind corn and make tortillas, and mind the babies—that is what girls are for. But boys—boys will be menand—" But here it seemed to occur to him that perhaps he was saying too much, and he became silent again.

José had listened thoughtfully, and when Pancho finished he sighed a little and made a soft little "ting-ting-a-ting-ting" on his guitar-strings. Then he jumped up and began to sing and dance, playing the guitar all the while. It was a song about the little dwarfs, and the children loved it.

José sang, — and every time he came to the words, —

he stooped down as he danced and made himself look as much like a dwarf as he possibly could.

When he had finished the Dwarf Song, José tucked his guitar under his arm, and bowed politely to Doña Teresa and Pancho.

"Adios!" he said. "May you rest well."

"Adios, adios!" shouted all the children.

And Pancho and Doña Teresa and the Twins replied: "Adios! God give you sweet sleep."

Then José and the children went away, and the tinkle of the guitar grew fainter and fainter in the distance. When they could no longer hear it, Doña Teresa went into the cabin, unrolled the mats, and laid out the pillows, and soon the Twins and their father and mother were all sound asleep on their hard beds.

When at last everything was quiet, the red rooster came stepping round from behind the house, and looked at the dying coals of the fire as if he wondered whether they were good to eat. He seemed to think it best not to risk it, however, for he flew up into the fig tree once more and settled himself for the night.

IV

TONIO'S BAD DAY

I

IT is hard for us to understand how they tell what season it is in a country like Mexico, where there is no winter, and no snow except on the tops of high mountains, and where flowers bloom all the year round.

Tonio and Tita can tell pretty well by the way they go to school. During the very hot dry weather of April and May there is vacation. In June, when the rainy season begins, school opens again. Then, though the rain pours down during some part of every day or night, in between times the sky is so blue, and the sunshine so bright, and the air so sweet, that the Twins like the rainy season really better than the dry.

If you should pass the open door of their school some day when it is in session, you would hear a perfect Babel of voices all talking at once and saying such things as this,—only they would say them in Spanish instead ofEnglish,—

"The cat sees the rat. Run, rat, run. Two times six is thirteen, two times seven is fifteen" (I hope you'd know at once that that was wrong). "Mexico is bounded on the north by the United States of America, on the east by the Gulf of Mexico, on the west by the Pacific Ocean, on the ... Cortez conquered Mexico in 1519 and brought the holy Catholic religion to Mexico. The Church is ..."

Then perhaps you would clap your hands on your ears and think the whole school had gone crazy, but it would only mean that in Mexico the children all study aloud. The sixth grade is as high as any one ever goes, and most of them stop at the fourth.

Señor Fernandez thinks that is learning enough for any peon, and as it is his school, and his teacher, and his land, of course things have to be as he says.

Pancho asked the priest about it one day. He said: "I should like to have Tonio get as much learning as he can. Learning must be a great thing. All the rich and powerful people seem to have it. Perhaps that is what makes them rich and powerful."

But the priest shook his head and said, "Tonio needs only to know how to be good, and obey the Church, and to read and write and count a little. More knowledge than that would make him unhappy and discontented with his lot. You do not wish to make him unhappy. Contentment with godliness is great gain. Is it not so, my son?"

The priest called everybody, even Señor Fernandez himself, "my son," unless he was speaking to a girl or a woman, and then he said, "my daughter."

Pancho scratched his head as if he were very much puzzled by a good many things in this world, but he only said, "Yes, little father," very humbly, and went away to mend the gate of the calves' corral.

II

I am not going to tell you very much about the Twins' school, because the Twins didn't care so very much about it themselves.

But I am going to tell you about one particular day, because that day a great deal happened to Tonio. Some of it wasn't at all pleasant, but you will not be surprised at that when I explain the reason why.

A good many months had passed by since San Ramon's Day, and it was a bright beautiful spring morning, when the Twins left their little adobe hut to go to school.

They had to be there at half past eight, and as the schoolhouse was some distance down the road and there were a great many interesting things on the way, they started rather early.

Doña Teresa gave them two tortillas apiece, rolled up with beans inside, to eat at recess, and Tonio wrapped them in a cloth and carried them in his hat just the way Pancho carried his lunch, only there was no chile sauce, this time. Doña Teresa waved good-bye to them from the trough where she was grinding her corn.

The air was full of the sweet odor of honeysuckle blossoms, and the roadsides were gay with flowers, as the Twins walked along. The birds were flying about getting material for their nests, and singing as if they would split their little throats.

Sheep were grazing peacefully in a pasture beside the road, with their lambs gamboling about them. In a field beyond, the goats were leaping up in the air and butting playfully at each other, as if the lovely day made them feel lively too. Calves were bleating in the corrals, and away off on the distant hillside the children could see cows moving about, and an occasional flash of red when a vaquero rode along, his bright serape flying in the sun.

Farther away there were blue, blue mountain-peaks crowned with glistening snow, and from one of them a faint streak of white smoke rose against the blue of the sky. It was a beautiful morning in a beautiful world where it seemed as if every one was meant to be happy and good.

The school was not far from the gate where José, the gate-keeper, sat all day, waiting to open and close the gate for cowboys as they drove the cattle through.

The Twins stopped to speak to José, and just then on a stone right beside the gate Tonio saw a little green lizard taking a sun bath. He was about six inches long and he looked like a tiny alligator.

Tonio crept up behind him very quietly and as quick as a flash caught him by the tail. Just then the teacher rang the bell, and the Twins ran along to join the other children at the schoolhouse door, but not one of them, not even Tita herself, knew that Tonio had that green lizard in his pocket!

Tonio didn't wear any clothes except a thin white cotton suit, and he could feel the lizard squirming round in his pocket. Tonio didn't like tickling, and the lizard tickled like everything.

As they came into the schoolroom, the boys took off their hats and said, "God give you good day," to the Señor Maestro—that is what they called the teacher.

Then they hung their hats on nails in the wall, while the girls curtsied to the teacher and went to their seats.

When they were all in their places and quiet, the Señor Maestro stood up in front of the school, and raised his hand. At once all the children knelt down beside their seats. The Maestro knelt too, put his hands together, bowed his head, and said a prayer. He was right in the middle of the prayer when the lizard tickled so awfully in Tonio's pocket that Tonio, — I really hate to have to tell it, but facts are facts, — Tonio laughed — aloud!

Then he was so scared, and so afraid he would laugh again if the lizard kept on tickling, that he put his hand in his pocket and took it out. Kneeling in front of Tonio was a boy named Pablo, and the bare soles of his feet were turned up in such a way that Tonio just couldn't help dropping the lizard on to them.

The lizard ran right up Pablo's leg, inside his cotton trousers, and Pablo let out a yell like a wild Indian on the warpath, and began to act as if he had gone crazy.

He jumped up and danced about clutching his clothes, and screaming! The Señor Maestro and the children were perfectly amazed. They couldn't think what ailed Pablo until, all of a sudden, the green lizard dropped on the floor out of his sleeve and scuttled as fast as it could toward the girls' side of the room. Then the girls screamed and stood on their seats until the lizard got out of sight.

Nobody knew where it had gone, until the Señor Maestro suddenly fished it out of a chink in the adobe wall and held it up by the tail.

"Who brought this lizard into the schoolroom?" he asked.

Tonio didn't have to say a word. I don't know how they could be so sure of it, but all the children pointed their fingers at Tonio and said, "He did."

The Maestro said very sternly to Tonio, "Go out to the willow tree and bring me a strong switch," Tonio went.

He went very slowly and came back with the willow switch more slowly still.

I think you can guess what happened next—I hope you can, for I really cannot bear to tell you about it. When it was over Tonio was sent home, while all the other children sat straight up in their seats, looking so hard at their books that they were almost cross-eyed, and studying their lessons at the top of their lungs.

If you had asked them then, they would every one have told you that they considered it very wrong to bring lizards to school, and that under no circumstances would they ever think of doing such a thing.

III

Tonio walked slowly down the road toward his home. He didn't cry, but he looked as if he wished he could just come across somebody else who was doing something wrong! He'd like to teach him better.

When José saw him, he called out to him, "Is school out?"

"No," said Tonio. "I am," and he never said another word to José.

He had the willow switch in his hand. The Maestro had given it to him, "to remember him by," he said. Tonio felt pretty sure he could remember him without it, but he switched the weeds beside the road with it as he walked along, and there was some comfort in that.

At last he remembered that he had a luncheon in the crown of his hat. He sat down beside the road and ate all four tortillas and every single bean. Then he went home. His mother was not in the house when he got there.

Jasmin came frisking up to Tonio and jumped about him and licked his hand. It seemed strange to Tonio that even a dog could be cheerful in such a miserable world. He took his lasso down from the wall and went out again with Jasmin.

The cat was lying back of the house in the sunshine asleep. Tonio pointed her out to Jasmin and he sent her up the fig tree in a hurry. Then Jasmin chased the hens. He drove the red rooster right in among the beehives, and when the bees came out to see what was the matter they chased Jasmin instead of the rooster, and stung him on the nose. Jasmin ran away yelping to dig his nose in the dirt, and Tonio went on by himself through the woods.

Soon he came to the stepping-stones that led across the river to the goat-pasture, and there he met José's son and another boy.

"Hello, there! Where are you going?" Tonio called to them.

"We aren't going; we've been," said José's son, whose name was Juan. The other boy's name was Ignacio.

"Well, where have you been then?" said Tonio.

"Down to the lake hunting crabs. We didn't find any," they said.

You see there is no law in Mexico that every child must go to school, and the parents of Juan and Ignacio didn't make them go either, so they often stayed away.

"What's the reason you're not in school?" Juan said to Tonio. "I thought your father always made you go."

"Well," said Tonio, "I—I—hum—well—I thought I would rather play bull-fight up in the pasture! I've got an old goat up there trained so he'll butt every time he sees me. Come along."

The three boys crossed on the stepping-stones, and ran up the hill on the other side of the river to the goat-pasture.

There was a growing hedge of cactus plants around the goat-pasture. This kind of cactus grows straight up in tall, round spikes about as large around as a boy's leg, and higher than a man's head. The spikes are covered with long, stiff spines that stick straight out and prick like everything if you run into them. The only way to get through such a fence is to go to the gate, so the boys ran along until they came to some bars. They opened the bars (and forgot to put them up again) and went into the pasture.

IV

When they got inside the pasture the boys looked about for the goat. This goat was quite a savage one, and was kept all by himself in a small field. It did not take them long to find him. He was grazing quietly in the shadow of a mesquite tree. As Tonio had the only lasso there was, he knew he could have the game all his own way, so he said, —

"I'll take the first turn with the lasso, Ignacio; you wave your red serape at the goat while Juan stirs him up from behind."

The goat had his head down, eating grass, and did not notice the boys until suddenly Juan split the air behind him with a fearful roar and prodded his legs with a stick.

"Ah, Toro!" roared Juan at the top of his lungs just as he had heard the matadors do at a real bull-fight, and at the same moment Ignacio shook out his red serape.

The goat looked up, saw Tonio and the red serape, and immediately stood up on his hind legs. Then he came down with a thump on his fore feet, put his head down, and ran at Ignacio like a bullet from a gun. Ignacio waved the serape and shouted, and when the goat got very near, he jumped to one side as he had seen the matadors do, and the goat butted with all his might right into the serape.

When he struck the serape his horn went through one end of it. Ignacio had hold of the other end and before he knew what had happened he was rolling backward down a little slope into a pool of water which was the goat's drinking-place.

Meanwhile the goat went bounding about the pasture with the serape hanging from one horn. Every few minutes he would stamp on it and paw it with his fore feet. Ignacio picked himself out of the water, and then all three boys began a wild chase to get back the serape. It would be a sad day for Ignacio if he went home without it.

Serapes are the most valuable things there are in a peon's hut, and were never intended to be used by goats in this way.

Tonio couldn't lasso the goat because the serape covered his horns, so the boys all tried to snatch off the serape as the goat went galloping past, but every time they tried it the goat butted at them, and they had to run for their lives.

At last the goat stood up on his hind legs and came down on the serape so hard that there was a dreadful tearing sound, and there was the serape torn clear in two and lying on the ground!

When his horns were free, the goat looked around for the boys. He was a very mad goat, and when he saw them he went for them like an express train. Juan ran one way, and Ignacio ran the other. Tonio was a naughty boy, but he wasn't a coward. He kept his lasso whirling over his head, and as the goat came by, out flew the loop and dropped over his horns!

The goat was much stronger than he, but Tonio braced back with all his might and held on to the rope. Then began a wild dance! The goat went bounding around the pasture with Tonio at the other end of the rope bouncing after him.

It was a sight to see, and Juan and Ignacio were not the only ones who saw it either.

V

Señor Fernandez was going by on his fine black horse, and when he heard the yells of the boys he rode up to the pasture to see what was going on. He was right beside the bars when the goat and Tonio came tearing through.

The goat jumped over the bars that the boys had left down, but Tonio caught his foot and fell down, and the goat jerked the rope out of his hands and went careering off over the fields and was soon out of sight.

Tonio sat up all out of breath and looked at Señor Fernandez. Señor Fernandez looked at Tonio. Juan and Ignacio were nowhere to be seen. They were behind bushes in the goat-pasture, and they were both very badly scared.

"Well," said Señor Fernandez at last, "what have you been doing?"

"Just playing bull-fight a little," Tonio answered in a very small voice.

"Didn't you know that was my goat?" said Señor Fernandez severely. "What business have you driving it mad like that? Get up."

Tonio got up. He was stiff and sore all over. Moreover, his hands were all skinned inside, where the rope had pulled through.

"Were you alone?" asked Señor Fernandez.

"Not—very—" stammered Tonio.

"Where are the other boys?" demanded the Señor Fernandez.

"I d—don't know," gasped poor Tonio. "I—I don't see them anywhere." (Tonio was looking right up into the top of the cactus hedge when he said this, so I am quite sure he spoke the truth.)

"Humph," grunted Señor Fernandez. "Go look for them."

Tonio began to hunt around stones and bushes in the pasture with Señor Fernandez following right behind on his horse. It wasn't long before he caught a glimpse of red. It was the pieces of the serape, which Ignacio had picked up. Tonio pointed it out, and Señor Fernandez galloped to it and brought out the two culprits. Then he marched the three boys back to the village in front of his horse, Tonio with his blistered hands and torn clothes, Juan with bumps that were already much swollen, and Ignacio wet as a drowned rat and carrying the rags of the serape.

When they got back to the river they found Doña Teresa there washing out some clothes. When she saw them coming she stopped rubbing and looked at them. She was perfectly astonished. She supposed, of course, that Tonio was in school.

"Here, Doña Teresa, is a very bad boy," Señor Fernandez said to her. "He has been chasing my goat all around the pasture and lassoing it, and he left the bars down and they are broken besides, and no one knows where the goat is by this time. I'll leave him to you, but I want you to make a thorough job of It."

He didn't say just what she should make a thorough job of, but Tonio hadn't the smallest doubt about what he meant. Doña Teresa seemed to understand too.

Señor Fernandez rode on and left Tonio with his mother while he took the other two boys to their homes. What happened there I do not know, but when she and Tonio were alone I do know that Doña Teresa said sternly, "Go bring me a strong switch from the willow tree," and that Tonio thought, as he went for it, that there were more willow trees in the world than were really needed.

And I know that when Doña Teresa had done "IT" — whatever it was that Señor Fernandez had asked her to do thoroughly — Tonio ffelt that it would be a very long time before he took any interest in either lizards or goats again.

That evening Pancho went out with Pinto and hunted up the goat and put him back in the pasture and brought home Tonio's lasso, and when he hung it up on the nail he said to Tonio, "I think you're too young to be trusted with a lasso. Let that alone for two weeks."

That was the very worst of all. To be told that he was too young! Tonio went out and sat down under the fig tree and thought perhaps he'd better run away.

But pretty soon Tita came out and sat down beside him and told him she was sure he never meant any harm about the lizard, and his mother washed his skinned hands and put oil on then, and brought him some molasses to eat on his tortillas just as if she still loved him in spite of everything.

So Tonio went to bed quite comforted, and that was the end of the day.

V

JUDAS ISCARIOT DAY

I

ONE day, later in spring, in the week just before Easter, Doña Teresa got ahead of the red rooster. It happened in this way. Early in the morning, when everything was still as dark as a pocket, and not a single rooster in the neighborhood had yet thought of crowing, Doña Teresa woke up and lighted a candle. Then see went over to the Twins' mat and held up her candle so she could look at them. They were both sound asleep.

"Wake up, my lambs," said Doña Teresa. But her lambs didn't wake up. Doña Teresa shook them gently. "Wake up, dormice! Don't you know this is Judas Iscariot Day, and you are all going to town? Come, we are going in Pedro's boat, and he has to start early."

Tita began to rub her eyes, and Tonio was sitting up with both of his wide open the moment Doña Teresa said the word "boat." They bounced out in a minute, and they even washed without being told, and they used soap, too!

Pancho was roused by the noise they made. He got up at once and went to attend to the donkey and to Pinto. When he opened the door the gleam of Doña Teresa's candle woke the red rooster. He began to crow, and then all the other roosters crowed, and almost right away candles were glimmering in every hut in the village and every one was up and getting ready to start to town.

Everybody was going. Some were going on horseback and some on donkeys; more were walking, and as it was many miles from the hacienda to the town it was necessary to start very early.

The quickest way to go was by boat, but, of course, not every one could go that way because there were not enough boats. Pedro's boat went back and forth every day between the hacienda and the town, carrying wood and all kinds of supplies. He was a friend of Pancho's and that was how they were so fortunate as to be invited to go with him.

Doña Teresa got breakfast very quickly, and while they were eating it they heard a voice calling, "Here, buy your Judases — at six and twelve cents — your Judases."

"There comes the Judas-seller. Run, children, run," cried Doña Teresa. "You may each have twelve cents and you may buy two little ones or one big one, as you like."

The Judas-seller had a long branch cut from a tree, with little twigs growing out of it. On each twig hung a "Judas." They were small dolls, with sticky pink-painted faces and sticky black-painted hair, and they were dressed in tissue paper. The hands of the Judases were stuck straight out on each side and from one hand to the other there was a string stretched. Fire-crackers were hung along on this string. When these fire-crackers go off, one after another, they set fire to the Judas and burn him up.

You remember that long years ago, when Jesus was on earth, He was betrayed by a man named Judas Iscariot, who sold Him to his enemies for thirty pieces of silver. In Mexico, Judas Iscariot Day is kept in remembrance of this, and all the Judases which the people buy and burn up are to show how very wicked they believe the real Judas to have been.

But the Judas dolls didn't look the least bit as the real Judas must have looked. Some of them were made to look like Mexican donkey-boys and some like water-carriers, while others represented priests, or policemen, or cowboys.

Tita couldn't make up her mind whether to buy a donkey-boy or a policeman. But Tonio found what he wanted right away. It was a "Judas" made like a thin young school-teacher! Tonio thought it looked like the Señor Maestro, and he thought it would be very pleasant to see him burn up,and so, though he cost twelve cents, he bought him at once.

II

When Pancho and Doña Teresa and the Twins were ready they went in a little procession to the lake-shore. They found Pedro with his wife and baby and Pablo already there.

This was the very same Pablo on whose feet Tonio had put the lizard. He was Pedro's son.

Pedro was loading the boat with bundles of reeds. They were the reeds used for weaving the petates or sleeping-mats. The reeds grew all about the lake, but the people in the town could not easily get them, so Pedro had gathered a supply to sell to them.

The boat was quite large. It had one sail and there was a thatched roof of reeds over the back part of it. It was too large to bring into the shallow water near the shore, so Pedro had rolled up his white trousers and was wading back and forth from the boat to the beach, carrying a bundle of reeds each time and stowing it away under the thatch.

Pancho at once took off his sandals, rolled up his trousers, and began to help carry the bundles, while Doña Teresa and the Twins sat on the sand with Pablo and the baby and their mother.

There was a large sack of sweet potatoes lying on the sand beside Pedro's wife. You could tell they were sweet potatoes because the bundle was so knobby. Besides Tonio felt of them.

"What are you going to do with your sweet potatoes?" asked Doña Teresa.

"I'm going to cook them in molasses and sell them," said Pedro's wife. "I shall sit under an awning and watch the fun and turn a penny at the same time. The baby is too heavy to carry round all day, anyway."

"I'll help you," said Doña Teresa. "Very likely I shall be glad enough to sit down somewhere myself before the day is over."

"Pedro made me a little brasero out of a tin box," said his wife, "and I have a bundle of wood right here, and the syrup and the dishes, all ready."

When the reeds had all been put on board, Pancho took Tonio in his arms and Pedro took Pablo, and they tossed them into the boat as if they had been sacks of meal. The boys scrambled under the covered part and out to the bow at once, and Pablo got astride the very nose of the boat and let his feet hang over.

Then Pedro lifted Tita in.

It was more of a job to get the mothers aboard, for Pedro's wife was fat, and he was a small man. Pedro shook his head when he looked at his wife, then he took off his sombrero, and scratched his head. At last he said, "I think I'll begin with the baby."

He took the baby and waded out to the boat and handed her to Tita, then he went back to shore and took another look at his wife. "It'll take two of us," he said to Pancho.

"I'm your man," said Pancho bravely. "I can lift half of her."

So Pedro and Pancho made a chair with their arms, and Pedro's wife sat on it, and put her arms around their necks, and they waded out with her into the water.

They got along beautifully until they reached the side of the boat and undertook to lift her over the edge. Then there came near being an awful accident, for Pedro's foot slipped on a slimy stone and he let her down on one side so that one of her feet went into the water.

"Holy mother!" screamed Pedro's wife. "They are going to drown me!"

She waved her arms about and jounced so that Pancho almost dropped the other foot in too, but just in time Pedro shouted, "One, two, three, and over she goes," and as he said over, he and Pancho gave a great heave both together, and in she went all in a heap beside Tita and the baby.

While she crawled under the awning and settled herself with the baby and stuck her foot out in the sunshine to dry, Pancho and Pedro went back for Doña Teresa. She wasn't very stout so they got her in without any trouble.

They put in the brasero and all the other things, and last of all Pancho and Pedro climbed on board themselves, hoisted the sail, and pushed off. Luckily the breeze was just right, and they floated away over the blue water at about the time of day that you first begin to think of waking up.

III

Even with a good breeze it took nearly an hour to sail across the lake. If they hadn't been in such a hurry to see the fun in town, the Twins and Pablo would have wished to have it take longer still.

Far away across the lake they could see the town with its little bright-colored adobe houses and the spire of the church standing up above the tree-tops.

As they drew nearer and nearer, they could see a bridge, and people passing over it, and flags flying, and then they turned into a river which ran through the town, where there were many other boats.

It took some time to find a good place to tie the boat, but at last it was done, and the whole party went ashore and started up the street toward the open square in the middle of the town.

Pedro and Pancho went ahead, each carrying three bundles of reeds on his back. Then came Pedro's wife with the bag of sweet potatoes, while Doña Teresa carried the baby. Pablo had the brasero and the wood, and Tonio and Tita brought up the rear with the molasses jug, the cooking-dishes, and their Judases all carefully packed together.

"Now, mind you, Tonio," said Doña Teresa as the procession started, "don'tyou get to watching everything in the street and forget that jug of molasses."

It was pretty hard to keep your mind on a jug when there were so many wonderful things to see. In the first place there was the street itself. No one had ever seen it so gay! Strings had been stretched back and forth across the street from the flat tops of the houses on either side, and from these strings hung thousands of tissue-paper streamers and pennants in all sorts of gorgeous colors.

The houses in Mexican towns are close to the street-line and stand very near together. They are built around a tiny open space in the center called a patio. The living-rooms open on the patio, so all that can be seen of a house from the street is a blank wall with a doorway, and perhaps a window or two with little balconies. Sometimes, if the door is open, there are glimpses of plants, flowers, and bird-cages in the little patio.

Pablo and Tonio and Tita had their hands full, but they kept their eyes open, and their mouths too. They seemed to feel they could see more that way.

It was not very long before they came to the public square or plaza of the town, and there on one side was the church whose spire they had seen from the boat.

On the other side was the market-place, and in the center of the square there was a fountain. In another place there was a gayly painted band-stand with the red, white, and green flag of Mexico flying over it.

There were beds of gay geraniums at each corner of the square, and large trees made a pleasant shade where people could sit and watch the crowds, or listen to music, if the band were playing.

Pedro and Pancho went straight across the street to the market side. There were rows of small booths there, and already many of them were occupied by people who had things to sell. There were peanut-venders, and pottery-sellers; there were women with lace and drawn work; there were foods of all kinds, and flowers, and birds in cages, and chickens in coops or tied up by the legs, and geese and ducks, — in fact, I can't begin to tell you all the things there were for sale in that market.

Pedro found a stall with an awning over it and took possession at once. He and Pancho put down the bundles of reeds in a pile, and his wife sat on them. Pedro placed the brasero on the ground in front of her, and the sweet potatoes by her side. Pablo put down the wood, and Doña Teresa put the baby into her arms. Tita gave her the cooking-dishes, and Tonio was just going to hand her the jug, when bang-bang-bang! — three fire-crackers went off one right after the other almost in his ear! Tonio jumped at least a foot high, and oh — the jug! It accidentally tipped over sideways, and poured a puddle of molasses right on top of the baby's head!

It ran down his cheek, but the baby had the presence of mind to stick his tongue out sideways and lick up some of it, so it wasn't all wasted.

Doña Teresa said several things to Tonio while the baby was being mopped up. Tonio couldn't see why they should mind it if the baby didn't.

At last Doña Teresa finished by saying to the Twins and Pablo, "Now you run round the square and have a good time by yourselves, only see that you don't get into any more mischief; and come back when you're hungry."

Pedro and Pancho had already gone off by themselves, and as they didn't say where they were going I can't tell you anything about it. I only know they were seen not long after in front of a pulque shop (pulque is a kind of wine) talking in low tones with a Tall Man on horseback, and that after that nobody saw them for a long time. It may be they went to a cock-fight, for there was a cock-fight behind the pulque shop and most of the other men went if they did not.

V

The Twins and Pablo with their precious Judases went to a bench near the fountain, and sat down to watch the fun. There were water-carriers filling their long earthen jars at the fountain; there were young girls in bright dresses who laughed a great deal; and there were young men in big hats and gay serapes who stood about and watched them.

There were more small boys than you could count. Twelve o'clock was the time that every one was supposed to set off his fire-crackers, and the children waited patiently until the shadows were very short indeed under the trees in the square and there had been one or two explosions to start the noise, then they tied their Judases up in a row to the back of the bench. They hung Tonio's Maestro in the middle, with Tita's donkey-boy on one side and the policeman on the other. Pablo's Judas was a policeman too, and they put him on the other side of the donkey-boy.

Then Pablo borrowed a match from a boy and set fire to the first cracker on his policeman. Fizz-fizz-bang! off went the first fire-cracker. Fizz-fizz-bang! off went the second one. When the third one exploded, the policeman whirled around on his string, one of his hands caught fire, and up he went in a puff of smoke.

They lighted the fuses on the donkey-boy and the other policeman, both at once, and last of all Tonio set fire to the Maestro Judas. He was the biggest one of all. While the fire-crackers went off in a series of bangs, Tonio jumped up and down and sang, "Pop goes the Maestro! Pop goes the

38

Maestro!" and Tita and Pablo thought that was so very funny that they hopped about and sang it too.

Just as the last fire-cracker went off and Tonio's Judas caught fire, and all three of them were dancing and singing at the top of their lungs, Tonio saw the Señor Maestro himself standing in front of the bench with his hands in his pockets, looking right at them!

Tonio shut his mouth so quickly that he bit his tongue, and then Pablo and Tita saw the Maestro and stopped singing too, and they all three ran as fast as they could go to the other side of the square and lost themselves in the crowd.

They stayed away for quite a long time. They were in the crowd by a baker's shop when a great big Judas which hung high overhead exploded and showered cakes over them. They each picked up a cake and then ran back to show their goodies to their mothers. They could hardly get near the booth at first, because there was quite a little crowd around it, but they squirmed under the elbows of the grown people, and right beside the brasero eating a piece of candied sweet potato, and talking to Doña Teresa, whom should they see but the Señor Maestro?

Tonio wished he hadn't come. He turned round and tried to dive back into the crowd again, but the Señor Maestro reached out and caught him by the collar and pulled him back. Tonio was very much frightened. He thought surely the Maestro had told his mother about "Pop goes the Maestro," and that very unpleasant things were likely to happen.

"Any way, there aren't any willow trees in the plaza," he said to himself. "That's one good thing."

But what really happened was this. The Maestro took three pennies out of his pocket, and said to Pedro's wife, "Please give me three pieces of your nice sweet potatoes for my three friends here!"

Pedro's wife was so busy with her cooking that she did not look up to see who his three friends were until she had taken the pennies and handed out the sweet potatoes. Then she saw Pablo and Tonio and Tita all three standing in a row looking very foolish.

She was quite overcome at the honor the Maestro had done her in buying sweet potatoes to give to her son, and Doña Teresa thought to herself, "They really must be very good and clean children to have the Maestro think so much of them as that." She thanked him, and Tonio and Tita and Pablo all thanked him.

After that there was a wonderful concert by a band all dressed in green and white uniforms with red braid, and at the end of the concert, it was four o'clock. Pedro's wife had sold all her sweet potatoes by that time and Pedro had sold all his reeds. Pancho had come back, the baby was sleepy, and every one was tired and ready to go home. So the whole party returned to the boat, this time without any heavy bundles except the baby to carry, and sailed away across the lake toward the hacienda.

Pancho and Doña Teresa and the Twins reached their little adobe hut just as the red rooster and the five hens and the turkey were flying up to their roost in the fig tree.

VI

THE ADVENTURE

I

ONE hot morning in early June, Doña Teresa took her washing down to the river, and Tonio and Tita went with her. They found Doña Josefa and Pedro's wife already there with their soiled clothes, and the three women had a good time gossiping together while they soaped the garments and scrubbed them well on stones at the water's edge.

Pablo and the Twins played in the water meanwhile, hunting mud turtles and building dams and trying to catch minnows with their hands.

At last Pablo's mother said to him, "Pablo, take this piece of soap and go behind those bushes and take a bath."

Then she went on telling Doña Teresa about a new pattern of drawn work she was beginning and forgot all about Pablo. Pablo disappeared behind the bush, and no one saw him again that day. He wasn't drowned, but it's my belief that he wasn't bathed either.

However, this story is not about Pablo. It's about Tonio and Tita, and what happened to them.

Doña Teresa said to them, "I wish you would get Tonto and go up the mountain beyond the pasture and bring down a load of wood. Take some lunch with you. You won't get lost, because Tonto knows the way home if you don't. Get all the ocote branches you can to burn in the brasero."

The Twins were delighted with this errand. It meant a picnic for them, so they ran back to the house and got Tonto and the luncheon and started away down the road as gay as two larks in the springtime.

They both rode on the donkey's back and they had Tonio's lasso with them. The luncheon was in Tonio's hat as usual. Tonio whistled for Jasmin, but he was nowhere to be found, so they started without him.

They crossed the goat-pasture, and this time Tonio did not forget to put up the bars. They passed the goat too, but Tonio rode right by and hoped the goat wouldn't notice him.

From the goat-pasture they turned into a sort of trail that led up the mountain-side, and rode on for two miles until they came to a thick wood. Here they dismounted and, leaving Tonto to graze comfortably by himself, began to search for ocote wood. Tonio had a machete stuck in his belt.

A machete is a long strong knife, and he used it to cut up the wood into small pieces. Then he tied it up in a bundle with his lasso to carry home on Tonto's back.

The children had such fun wandering about, gathering sticks, and looking for birds' nests that they didn't think a thing about time until they suddenly realized that they were very hungry. They had gone some distance into the wood, and quite out of sight of Tonto by this time.

II

They sat down on a fallen log and ate their lunch, and then they were thirsty.

"Let's find a brook and get a drink," said Tonio. "I know there must be one right near here."

They left their bundle of wood and walked for some distance searching for water, but no stream did they find. They grew thirstier and thirstier.

"It seems to me I shall dry up and blow away if we don't find it pretty soon," said Tita.

"I've almost found it, I think," answered Tonio. "It must be right over by those willow trees."

They went to the willow trees but there was no stream there.

"I think we'd better go back and get the wood and start home," said Tita. "We can get a drink in the goat-pasture."

"All right," said Tonio, and he led the way back into the woods.

They looked and looked for the bundle of sticks, but somehow everything seemed different.

"I'm sure it must have been right near here," said Tonio. "I remember that black stump. I'm sure I do, because it looks like a bear sitting up on his hind legs. Don't you remember it, Tita?"

But Tita didn't remember it, and I'm afraid Tonio didn't either, really, for the bundle of sticks certainly was not there. They hunted about for a long time, and at last Tonio said, "I think we'd better go back to Tonto; he may be lonesome."

But Tonto had disappeared too! Tonio was sure he knew just where he had left him, but when they got to the place he wasn't there, and it wasn't the place either! It was very discouraging.

At last Tonio said, "Well, anyway, Tonto knows the way home by himself. We'll just let him find his own way, and we'll go home by ourselves."

"All right," said Tita, and they started down the mountain-side.

They had walked quite a long way when Tita said, "I think we're high enough up so we ought to see the lake." But no lake was in sight in any direction.

Tita began to cry. "We-we-we're just as lost as we can be," she sobbed. "And you did it! You said you knew the way, and you didn't, and now we'll die of hunger and nobody will find us—I want to go home."

"Hush up," said Tonio. "Crying won't help. We'll keep on walking and walking and we'll just have to come to something, some time. And there'll be people there and they'll tell us how to go."

Tonio seemed so sure of this that Tita was a little comforted. They walked for a very long time—hours it seemed to her—before Tita spoke again.

Then she said, "There's a big black cloud, and the sun is lost in it, and it's going to rain, and we aren't anywhere at all yet!"

They had got down to level ground by this time and were walking through a great field of maguey plants. The maguey is a strange great century-plant that grows higher than a man's head. When it gets ready to blossom the center is cut out and the hollow place fills with a sweet juice which

Mexicans like to drink. Tonio knew this and thought perhaps he could get a drink in that way.

So he cut down a hollow-stemmed weed with his machete and made a pipe out of it. Then he climbed up on the plant that had been cut and stuck one end of his pipe into the juice, and the other into his mouth. When he had had enough, he boosted Tita up and she got a drink too. This made them feel better, and they walked on until they had passed the maguey plantation and were out in the open fields once more.

III

The sky grew darker and darker, and there were queer shapes all around them. Giant cacti with their arms reaching out like the arms of a cross loomed up before them. There were other great cacti in groups of tall straight spines, and every now and then a palm tree would spread its spiky leaves like giant fingers against the sky.

Suddenly there was a great clap of thunder, "It's the beginning of the rains," said Tonio.

"Shall we — shall we — be drowned — do you think?" wept Tita. "It's almost night."

Tonio was really a brave boy, but it is no joke to be lost in such country as that, and he knew it.

Tonio was almost crying, too, but he said, "I'll climb the first tree I can get up into and look around." He tried to make his voice sound big and brave, but it shook a little in spite of him.

Soon they came to a mesquite tree. There were long bean-like pods hanging from it. Tonio climbed the tree and threw down some pods. They were good to eat. Tita gathered them up in her rebozo, while Tonio gazed in every direction to see if he could see a house or shelter of any kind.

"I don't see anything but that hill over there," he called to Tita. "It is shaped like a great mound and seems to be all stone and rock. Perhaps if we could get up on top of it and look about we could tell where we are."

"Let's run, then," said Tita.

The children took hold of hands and ran toward the hill. There were cacti of all kinds around them, and as they ran, the spines caught their clothes. The hill seemed to get bigger and bigger as they came nearer to it, and it didn't look like any hill they had ever seen. It was shaped like a great pyramid and was covered with blocks of stone. There were bushes growing around the base and out of cracks between the stones. Tonio tried to climb up but it was so steep he only slipped back into the bushes, every time he tried.

"Oh, Tonio, maybe it isn't a hill at all," whispered Tita. "Maybe it's the castle of some awful creature who will eat us up!"

"Well, whatever it is he won't eat me up!" said Tonio boldly. "I'll stick a cactus down his throat and he'll have to cough me right up if he tries."

"I'll kick and scream so he'll have to cough me up too," sobbed Tita.

Just then there came a flash of lightning. It was so bright that the children saw what they hadn't noticed before. It was a hollow place in the side of the pyramid where a great stone had fallen out, and the dirt underneath had been washed away, leaving a hole big enough for them to crawl into, but it was far above their heads.

At last Tonio climbed into a small tree that grew beside it, bent a branch over, and dropped down into the hollow, holding to the branch by his hands.

Poor Tita never had felt so lonely in her whole life as she did when she saw Tonio disappear into that hole! In a minute he was out again and looking over the edge at her.

"It's all right. You climb up just as I did," he said.

Tita tied the mesquite pods in the end of her rebozo and threw it up to Tonio. Then she too climbed the little tree and dropped from the branch into the mouth of the tiny cave.

A hole in the side of a queer pyramid isn't exactly a cheerful place to be in during a storm, but it was so much better than being lost in a cactus grove that the children felt a little comforted.

The rain began to fall in great splashing drops, but they were protected in their rocky house. They ate the mesquite pods for their supper, and then Tonio said: "Of course, no one will find us to-night, so we'd better go to sleep. We'll play we are foxes. The animals and birds sleep in such places all the time and they're not afraid."

So they curled down in the corner of the cave, and, being very tired, soon fell asleep.

VII

WHILE THEY WERE GONE

I

MEANWHILE what do you suppose had been happening at home? When she had finished her washing and had dried the clothes on the bushes, Doña Teresa folded them and carried them back to the house, and began her ironing.

She didn't think much about the time because she was so busy with her work, but at last she felt hungry and glanced out at the shadow of the fig tree to see what time it was.

She was surprised to see the shadow already quite long and pointing toward the east.

"Well," thought she to herself, "I'll get myself something to eat, and by that time the children will be home and as hungry as two bears. I think I'll get something especially good for their supper."

She hummed a little tune as she worked, and every little while she glanced out the open door to see if they were not coming. By and by she noticed that the sky was overcast and then she heard a clap of thunder. It was the very same clap of thunder that had frightened the Twins in the cactus grove.

"The holy saints above us!" cried Doña Teresa aloud. "The children should have been home long ago. Where can they be!" She ran to the door just in time to see Tonto come ambling slowly into the yard alone and go to his own place in the shed.

Doña Teresa's eyes almost popped out of her head with surprise and fright. She threw on her rebozo and ran over to Pedro's hut. Pedro's wife was just examining Pablo's ears to see if he had really washed himself in the river, when Doña Teresa arrived, quite breathless, at the door.

"Whatever can be the reason that my children are not home?" she gasped. "You remember it was morning when I sent them after wood. They have not been seen since, and Tonto walked into the yard just now all alone, and

47

of course there's nothing to be got out of him! What can have happened to them?"

"Now, never you mind, like a sensible woman," said Pablo's mother soothingly. "They're playing along the way as likely as not and will be at your door before you are. Who should know better than myself the way children will forget the thing they're set to do."

She looked severely at Pablo as she said this, so I judge the examination of his ears had not been satisfactory.

Doña Teresa didn't wait to hear any more, but ran back home, and when the children still did not appear she walked down the road hoping to meet them.

The clouds grew blacker and blacker, and the rain began to fall. Doña Teresa called Jasmin, who had reappeared by this time, and gave him Tonio's shoes to smell of.

"Go find him, go find him," she cried.

Jasmin whined and looked anxious, but just then came a flash of lightning. Jasmin was afraid of lightning, so he crept into Tonto's stall with his tail between his legs and hid there until the storm was over.

II

At last it was time for Pancho to come home. Poor Doña Teresa kept her supper hot and waited anxiously to hear the sound of Pinto's hoofs, but no such sound came. Pancho would go with her, and together they would find their children, she was sure, but six o'clock and seven came, without either Pancho or the children.

It was quite dark when at last she put on her rebozo and ran as fast as she could to the priest's house. The door was opened by the priest's fat sister, who kept house for him.

"Oh, where is the padrecito?" Doña Teresa said to her. "I must see him."

"He is eating his supper," said the fat sister.

"Tell him I am in great trouble," sobbed Doña Teresa.

In a moment the priest appeared at the door, and Doña Teresa kissed the hand he stretched out to her, and told him her anxieties all in one breath.

The padrecito had just had his supper and was feeling very comfortable himself, so he told her he was sure that everything would come out all right. He patted Doña Teresa on the shoulder and said not to worry; that probably Pancho had had to stay to mend a fence somewhere, and the children—why, they had probably stopped to play!

"In pitch darkness and rain, holy father? It cannot be," Doña Teresa moaned.

"Well," said the priest, "if they are not here in an hour we will search for them, but they will surely come soon."

Doña Teresa had such faith in the priest that she went back home, intending to do just what he said, but when she got there she found Pedro's wife waiting for her.

The moment she saw Doña Teresa she cried out, "Has Pancho come?"

"No," sobbed Doña Teresa.

"Neither has Pedro," answered his wife. "I can't think what can be the matter. He never stays out so late as this—especially in a storm. Something dreadful has surely happened."

Doña Teresa told her what the priest had said, but neither one was willing to wait another minute, so they ran together in the rain to the other huts and told the news, and the men formed a searching-party at once.

They put on their grass coats to protect them from the rain, and started off in the darkness and wet, carrying lighted pine torches, and calling loudly, "Pancho—Pedro—Tonio—Tita," every few minutes.

While they were gone Pedro's wife left the baby and Pablo with a neighbor and asked her to send Pablo to the chapel if there should be any news. Then she and Doña Teresa went there to pray.

The chapel door was open and candles were burning on the little altar, as the two women crept in and knelt before the image of the Virgin and Child.

"O Holy Mother," sobbed Doña Teresa, "help us who are mothers, too!"

All night long they knelt on the chapel floor before the images, sobbing and praying, listening for footsteps that did not come, and promising many candles to be placed upon the altar, if only their dear ones could be restored to them.

It was long after the rain was over and the moon shining again that the weary search party returned to the village without any news of the wanderers.

VIII

THE SECRET MEETING

I

THE children, meanwhile, were sleeping soundly in their hard bed. They were so tired that they did not wake up even when a tiny stream of water broke through a crevice in the rocks and splashed down on Tonio's head. It ran off his hair just as the rain ran off the thatched roof of their little adobe hut.

About nine o'clock the rain stopped and the moon shone out from behind the clouds. An owl hooted; a fox ran right over the roof of their cave, making a soft pat-pat with his paws that would have frightened them if they had heard it, but they slept on.

At last, however, something did wake Tita. She sat up in terror. A flickering light that wasn't moonlight was dancing about the cave! It was so bright that she could see everything about them as plain as day.

She clutched Tonio, shook him gently, and whispered in his ear, "Tonio, Tonio, wake up."

Tonio stirred and opened his mouth, but Tita clapped her hand over it. She was so afraid he would make a noise. When he saw the flickering light Tonio almost shouted for joy, for he was sure that his father had found them at last.

The flickering light grew brighter. They heard the crackling of flames and men's voices, and saw sparks. Very quietly they squirmed around on their stomachs until they could peep out of the opening of their cave.

This is what they saw!

There on the ground a few feet in front of their hiding-place was a fire, and two men were beside it. Their horses were tied to bushes not far away. One of the men was broiling meat on the end of a stick. The smell of it made the children very hungry. The other man was drinking something hot from a cup. They both had guns, and the guns were leaning against the rocks just below the cave where the children were hidden.

The man who was standing up was tall and had a fierce black mustache. He had on a big sombrero, and under a fold of his serape Tonio could see a cartridge-belt and the handle of a revolver.

"It's the Tall Man that Father and Pedro were talking to in front of the pulque shop," whispered Tonio.

Tita was so frightened that she shook like a leaf and her teeth chattered.

Pretty soon the Tall Man spoke. "The others ought to be here soon," he said. "They'll see the fire. Put on a few more sticks and make it flame up more."

The other man gave a last turn to the meat, handed it stick and all to the Tall Man, and disappeared behind the bushes to search for wood.

He had not yet come back, when there was the sound of horses' feet, and a man rode into sight, dismounted, hitched his horse, and joined the Tall Man by the fire.

One by one others came, until there were ten men standing about and talking together in low tones. Last of all there was the thud-thud of two more horses and who should come riding into the firelight but Pancho on Pinto, and Pedro on another horse!

When they joined the circle, Tonio almost sprang up and shouted. He did make a little jump, but Tita clutched him and held him back. He loosened a pebble at the mouth of the cave by his motion and it clattered down over the rock. The man who had gone for the wood was just putting his load down by the fire when the pebble came rattling down beside him.

"What's that?" he said, and sprang for his rifle.

Tonio hastily drew in his head. The men all listened intently for a few minutes, and looked cautiously about them.

"It's nothing but a pebble," said the Tall Man at last. "No one will disturb us here. And if they should," —he tapped the handle of his revolver and smiled,—"we'd give them such a warm welcome they would be glad to stay with us—quietly—oh, very quietly!"

The other men grinned a little, as if they saw a joke in this, and then they all sat down in a circle around the fire.

II

Pancho and Pedro sat where the children could look right at them. The Tall Man was the only one who did not sit down. He stood up and began to talk.

"Well, men," he said. "I knew I could count on you! Brave fellows like you know well when a blow must be struck, and where is the true Mexican who was ever afraid to strike a blow when he knew that it was needed?

"We came of a race of fighters! And once Mexico belonged to them! Our Indian forefathers did not serve a race of foreign tyrants as we, their sons, do! Look about you on Mexico! Where in the whole world can be found such a land? The soil so rich that it yields crops that burden the earth, and mountains full of gold and silver and precious stones! And it is for this reason we are enslaved!

"If our land were less rich and less beautiful, if it bore no such crops, if its sunshine were not so bright, and its mountains yielded no such treasure, we should be free men to-day.

"But the world envied our possessions. You know how Cortez, long ago, came from Spain and when our forefathers met him with friendliness he slew men, women, and children, tore down their ancient temples, and set the churches of Spain in their places!

"The Spaniards turned our fathers from free and brave men into a conquered and enslaved people, and worst of all they mixed their hated blood with ours. From the days of Cortez until now in one way or another we have submitted to oppression, until the spirit of our brave Indian ancestors is almost dead within us!

"And for what do we serve these aristocrats? For the privilege of remaining ignorant! For the privilege of tilling their fields, which were once ours! For the privilege of digging our gold and silver and precious stones out of theirmines to make them rich! For the privilege of living in huts while they live in palaces! For the privilege of being robbed and beaten in the name of laws we never heard of and which we had no part in making, though this country is called a Republic! A Republic! — Bah! — A Republic where more than half the people cannot read! A Republic of cattle! A Republic where men like you work for a few pence a day, barely enough to keep your body and soul together — and even that pittance you must spend in stores owned by the men for whom you work!

"The little that you earn goes straight back into the pockets of your masters! Do you not see it? Do you not see if they own the land and the supplies they own you too? They call you free men — but are you free? What are you free to do? Free to starve if you will not work on their terms, or if you will not strike a blow for freedom. Are not my words true? Speak up and answer me! Are you satisfied? Are you free?"

III

The Tall Man stopped and waited for an answer. The fire flickered over the dark faces of angry men, and Pedro stirred uneasily as if he would like to say something.

"Speak out, Pedro. Tell us your story," said the Tall Man.

Pedro stood up and shook his fist at the fire. "Every word you speak is true," he said. "Who should know better than I? I had a small farm some miles from here, left me by my father. It was my own, and I tilled my land and was content. My father could not read, neither could I. No one told me of the laws.

"At last one day a rural rode to my house, and said, 'Pedro, why have you not obeyed the law? The law says that if you did not have your property recorded before a magistrate by the first of last month it should be taken from you and given to the State.'

"'But I have never heard of such a law,' I said to him. He answered, 'Ignorance excuses no man. Your farm belongs to the state.' And I and my family were turned out of the house in which I and my father before me had been born. All our neighbors were treated in the same way. In despair we went away to the hacienda of Señor Fernandez, and there we work for a pittance as you say. And our homes! That whole region was turned over by the President, not long after, to a rich friend of his, who now owns it as a great estate!

"Many of my old neighbors are now his peons — working for him on land that was once their own and that was taken from them by a trick — by a trick, I say," — his voice grew thick, and he sat down heavily in his place.

Another man, a stranger to Tonio, sprang to his feet. "Ah, if that were all!" he said; "but even in peonage we are not left undisturbed! It was only a year ago that I was riding into town on my donkey with some chickens to sell, when an officer stopped me and brought me before the Jefe Politico.

"'Why have you not obeyed the law?' said the magistrate. 'I know of no law that I have not obeyed,' I said. 'You may tell me that,' said the scoundrel, 'but to make me believe it is another matter. You must know very well that a law was passed not long ago that every peon must wear dark trousers if he wishes to enter a town.'

"'I have no dark trousers,' said I, 'and I have no money to buy them. I have worn such white trousers as these since I was a boy, as have all the men in this region.' 'That makes no difference to me,' he said; 'law is law.' I was put in prison and made to work every day on a bridge that the Government was building! I never saw my donkey or the chickens again. My wife did not know where I was for two weeks.

"While I was working on the bridge five other men whom I knew were seized and treated in the same way. It is my belief that there is no such law. They wanted workmen for that bridge and that was the cheapest way to get them!"

"Where are those other five men who were imprisoned, too? Have they no spirit?" It was the Tall Man who spoke.

"They have spirit," the man answered, "but they also have large families. They fear to leave them lest they starve. They are helpless."

"Say rather they are fools," said the Tall Man when the stranger sat down. "Why had they not the spirit like you to take things in their own hands — to revenge their wrongs? As for myself," he went on, "every one knows my story.

"The blood of my Indian ancestors was too hot in my veins for such slavery — by whatever name you call it. I broke away, and my name is now a terror in the region that I call mine.

"It is no worse to take by violence than by fraud. My land was taken from me by fraud. Very well, I take back what I can by violence. The rich call us bandits, but there is already an army of one thousand men waiting for you to join them, and we call ourselves Soldiers of the Revolution. We have risen up to get for ourselves some portion of what we have lost.

"Will you not join us? Our general is a peon like yourselves. He feels our wrongs because he has suffered them, and he fights like a demon to avenge them. Ride away to-night with me! You shall see something besides driving other people's cattle — and being driven like cattle yourselves!"

The Tall Man stopped talking and waited for an answer. No one spoke. The men gazed silently into the fire as if they were trying to think out something that was very puzzling.

The Tall Man spoke again. "Sons of brave ancestors, do you know where you are?" he said. "Do you know what this great pyramid is?" He pointed directly up toward the cave, and Tonio and Tita, who had listened to every word, instantly popped their heads out of sight like frightened rabbits.

"This stone mountain was built by your Indian ancestors hundreds of years ago. It is the burial-place of their dead. It is called the Pyramid of the Moon. Look at it! Have the Spaniards built anything greater? Mexico has many mighty monuments which show the glory which was ours before the Spaniards came.

"I have seen the ruins of great cities — cities full of stone buildings covered with wonderful carvings, all speaking of the magnificence of the days of Cuauhtemoc. Here in this place the souls of those brave ancestors listen for your answer. There are many people who do not know — who do not feel — who are content to be like the sheep on the hillside; but you, you know your wrongs, — come with us and avenge them!"

IV

The man who had gone for the wood now spoke. He took up one of the rifles. "See!" he said, "we have guns enough for you, and you have horses. It is time to start. The morning will soon be here."

The men rose slowly from their places around the fire. Tonio saw some of them glance fearfully around at the great Pyramid of the Moon in which they were hidden and furtively cross themselves. Then he heard his father's voice. It was the first time Pancho had spoken.

"I will go with you," said Pancho. "I am no sheep. I, too, have suffered many things. My wife is a strong woman. She will look after the children while I am gone. I have no fear for them."

When Tita heard her father say these dreadful words she almost screamed, but now Tonio clapped his hand over her mouth.

"Keep still," he whispered in her ear. "Those other men might kill us if they knew we were here and had heard everything."

Tita hid her face on her arms, and her whole body shook with sobs, but she did not make a sound—not even when she saw Pancho and Pedro ride away with the two men whom they had first seen by the fire.

Four of the other men went with them too. The ones who had made the sign of the cross did not go.

The children could catch only a few words of what they said when Pancho and Pedro and the others rode away, but it sounded like this: "—Our wives—our children—we shall not forget—by and by—perhaps in the spring—" And then they heard the voice of the Tall Man speaking very sharply.

"If you will not go with us, see that you keep silence," he said. "If any news of this gets about in this region we shall know whom to blame and to punish! We shall come back and we shall know," and then "Á dios—á dios—ádios—" and the hoof-beats of horses as they rode away, then silence again, and the moon sailing away toward the west, with only the glow of the dying coals to show that any one had been there at all.

57

When they were gone, the children wept together as if their hearts would break, but soon the birds began to sing, and the sky grew brighter and brighter in the east, and the coming of the sunshine comforted them.

When it was quite light they let themselves down out of their nest and warmed themselves over the coals. They had nothing to eat, of course, and they did not know which way to go. But Tonio had an idea.

"Father and Pedro came from this direction," he said, pointing toward the south, "and so the hacienda must be somewhere over that way."

V

They started bravely toward the south and had not gone far when they struck a rough road. Tonio stooped down and found the fresh prints of Pinto's hoofs in the mud.

"This is the way," he cried joyfully. "I'm sure of it."

They walked on and on, but they were too hungry to go very fast. By and by they sat down on a stone to rest. They had been there only a short time when they heard the beat of horses' hoofs, and galloping down a hill they saw two people on horseback. One was a lady. The other was a man.

The children watched them eagerly, and in a moment Tita sprang up and began to run towards them, shouting joyfully, "It's the Señorita Carmen!"

Then Tonio ran too. When Carmen saw the two wild little figures she shouted and waved her hand to them, and she and the mozo, or servant, who was on the other horse, galloped as fast as they could up the hill to meet them.

When they reached the children, Carmen sprang down from her horse and threw her bridle-rein to the mozo. Then she quickly opened a little bundle which he handed her, and gave the children each a drink of milk, and some food, and all the while she murmured comforting things to them.

"Poor little ones — poor little souls!" she said, patting them. "We have been looking for you, the mozo and I, since daybreak! Where have you been, my poor pigeons? Your mother is nearly wild with grief! Tell me, have you

58

seen anything of your father or Pedro? They have not been home either. We thought perhaps they might be searching for you too."

Tonio and Tita both had their hungry mouths so full they could not answer just then, but when the mozo had lifted Tita up on the horse behind Carmen, and had taken Tonio up on his own horse, and they were on their way home, they told Carmen and the mozo just how they got lost, only neither one said a single word about their father or Pedro, or the Tall Man, or the group they had seen around the fire.

They remembered what the Tall Man had said about coming back to punish any one who should tell of the secret meeting, and they remembered how fierce his voice sounded as he said it.

When at last they rode into the gate of the hacienda every one was so glad to see them that the Twins felt like heroes.

José waved his hat and shouted when he saw them coming, and Jasmin came tearing out to meet them with his tongue hanging out and his tail stuck straight out behind him like the smoke behind a fast locomotive.

The news spread quickly through the village, and all the boys and girls and the mothers came swarming out of their huts to greet them and to ask a thousand questions about where they had been.

The first one to reach them was Doña Teresa. She came running out of the chapel, with her rebozo flying out behind her almost like Jasmin's tail, and she clasped them in her arms and kissed them again and again and called them her lambs, her angels, her precious doves.

She kissed the hands of Carmen and thanked her, and then she ran back with the Twins to the chapel and made them say a prayer of thankfulness with her before the image of the Virgin.

VI

It was not until she had them all to herself in their little adobe hut that she made them tell her every word about their adventure. Of course they told their mother everything—about the fire and the Tall Man, and the guns, and what he said about coming back to punish any one who told.

Doña Teresa rocked back and forth on her knees and wiped her eyes on her apron as she listened to them, while at the same time she made them hot chocolate on the brasero.

As they were drinking it she said to them: "Listen, my children. I will tell you a secret. Promise me first that you will never, never tell what I am going to tell you now!"

The children promised.

Then Doña Teresa went on: "I am not wholly surprised at your father's disappearance. I knew he had seen the Tall Man. I knew it after Judas Iscariot's Day. The Tall Man talked then with him and Pedro and some others, and asked them to join the Revolution. I begged him on my knees not to go, but he said: 'If I go it is only to make things better for us all. I'm tired of this life. Peons might just as well be slaves.'"

"What is the Revolution?" asked Tonio.

"Oh, I don't know," sobbed Doña Teresa. "Your father says it is rising up to fight against wrongs and oppression. He says the Government is in league with the rich and powerful and even with the Church" — here Doña Teresa crossed herself — "to keep the poor people down, and to take away their land. He says the Revolution is going to give back the land to the people and give them a better chance.

"That's what the Tall Man told him. But to me it looks like just adding to our poverty. Here at least we have a roof over our heads, and food, such as it is, and I could be content. What good it will do any one to go out and get shot I cannot see, — but then, of course, I am only a woman." She finished with a sob.

"Father told the Tall Man that you were a strong woman and that he had no fear for us because you would look after us while he is gone," said Tita.

"And so I will, my lamb," said Doña Teresa. "It is not for nothing that I am the best ironer and the best cook on the hacienda. You shall not suffer, my pigeons. But you must help me. You must never, never, NEVER tell any one where your father has gone. Señor Fernandez would be angry. It might injure your father very much. We must be silent, and work hard to make up for his absence. I shall tell Pedro's wife. She knows about the Tall Man, and it was the first thing we both thought of when your father and Pedro did not come home last night. But Pablo doesn't know a thing about it, and he must not know. I'm afraid Pablo couldn't keep a secret!"

This made the Twins feel very grown up and important. Perhaps after all their father would come back and things would be better for them all, they thought. He probably knew best, for was he not a man? And so they lay down on their hard beds, warmed and fed and comforted, and slept, while Doña Teresa went over and told Pedro's wife all that the Twins had told her.

IX

CHRISTMAS AT THE HACIENDA

I

DAYS and weeks and months went by and still there was no news of the wanderers. Doña Teresa worked hard at her washing and cooking, and with the goat's milk and the eggs managed to get enough to feed the Twins and herself. But the time seemed long and lonely, and she spent many hours before the image of the Virgin in the chapel, praying for Pancho's safe return. She even paid the priest for special prayers, and out of her scanty earnings bought candles to burn upon the altar. At last the Christmas season drew near.

The celebration of Christmas lasts for more than a whole week in Mexico. Every evening for eight evenings before Christmas all the people in the village met together and marched in a procession all round the hacienda. This procession is called the Pasada.

Everybody marched in it, and when on the first evening they came to the priest's house, he came out and stood beside his door and gave to each person a lighted candle, which his fat housekeeper handed out to him.

Then while all the people stood there with the candles shining like little stars, he told them this story, to remind them of the meaning of the procession: —

"Listen, my children," he said. "Long years ago, just before our Saviour was born, Mary, his mother, went with Joseph, her husband, from the little town of Nazareth, where they lived, into Judæa. They had to make this journey because a decree had been passed that every one must be taxed.

"Joseph and the Blessed Mother of our Lord were always obedient to the law, so they went at once to Bethlehem in Judæa, which was the place where their names had to be enrolled. My children, you also should obey in all things, as they did. Discontent and rebellion should have no place in your lives, — as it had no place in theirs.

"When Joseph and Mary reached Bethlehem they found the town so full of people, who had come from far and near for this purpose, that there was no room for them in the inn. For eight days they wandered about seeking a place to rest and finding none.

"At last, on the ninth day, they were so weary that they took shelter in a stable with the cattle, and there on that night our Blessed Saviour was born. They were poorer than you, my children, for they had no place to lay their heads, and the Queen of Heaven had only a manger in which to cradle her newborn son. It is to commemorate their wanderings that you make your Pasada."

When the priest had finished the story the people all marched away carrying their candles and singing. Each night they marched and sang in this way until at last it was Christmas Eve.

Doña Teresa and the twins went to bed early that night because there was to be high mass in the little chapel at midnight. Doña Teresa slept with one eye open, fearing she might be late, and a few minutes before twelve she was up again.

She washed the Twins' faces to wake them, and then they all three walked in the starlight to the little chapel near the Big House. The altar was blazing with lights, and the floor was covered with the dark figures of kneeling men and women, as the mother and children went in out of the darkness and found a place for themselves in a corner near the door.

When the service was over, Doña Teresa hurried home to set the house in order and to prepare the Christmas dinner for the Twins. She had made up her mind that the red rooster must surely be caught and cooked, because she wanted to keep the turkey until Pancho should be at home to share in the feast.

She had planned it all carefully. "It will be quite easy to creep up under the fig tree while the red rooster is asleep and seize him by the legs," she said to the Twins as they walked home from the chapel. "Only you must be very quiet indeed or he will wake up and crow. You know he is a light sleeper!"

They slipped through the gate and into the yard as quietly as they could. They reached the fig tree without making a single sound and Doña Teresa peered cautiously into the dark branches.

She saw a large shadow at the end of the limb where the red rooster always slept and, stretching her hand very stealthily up through the branches, she suddenly grabbed him by the legs — or she thought she did.

But the owner of the legs gobbled loud enough to wake every one in the village, if they hadn't been awake already!

"It's the turkey, after all," gasped Doña Teresa. Just then there was a loud crow from the roof, and they saw the silhouette of the red rooster making all haste to reach the ridge-pole and fly down on the other side.

Doña Teresa was in despair, but she held on to the turkey. "That rooster is bewitched," she said.

Just then the turkey stopped gobbling long enough to peck vigorously at Tonio, who came to help his mother, and Doña Teresa said, "Well, then, we'll eat the turkey, anyway, though I had hoped to wait until your father gets home. But we must have something for our Christmas dinner, and there's no telling when we shall see the red rooster again."

"I shouldn't want to eat the red rooster, anyway," said Tita. "He seems just like a member of the family."

And so the Christmas dinner was settled that way.

The turkey wasn't the only thing they had. There was rice soup first, then turkey, and they had frijoles, and tortillas, of course, and bananas beside, and all the sweet potatoes cooked in syrup that they could possibly hold. It took Doña Teresa so long to cook it all on her little brasero that she didn't go back to bed at all, though the Twins had another nap before morning.

They had their dinner early, and when they had finished eating, Tita said, "We must give a Christmas dinner to the animals too."

So Tonio brought alfalfa in from the field on purpose for Tonto, and the red rooster appeared in time to share with the hens twice as much corn as was usually given them. The cat had a saucer of goat's milk, and Tonio even found some bones for Jasmin, so every single one of them had a happy Christmas Day.

At dusk when candles began to glimmer about the village and all the people were getting ready for the Christmas Pasada, Doña Teresa said to the Twins, "You take your candles and run along with Pablo. I am going to the chapel." And while all the other people marched round among the cabins, singing, she stayed on her knees before the image of the Virgin, praying once more for Pancho's safe return.

When they reached the priest's house, the priest himself joined the procession and marched at the head of it, bearing in his hands large wax images of the Holy Family. Behind him came Lupito, the young vaquero who had taken Pancho's place on the hacienda, with his new wife, and following them, if you had been there, you might have seen Pedro's wife and baby, and Rafael and José and Doña Josefa, and Pablo and the Twins with Juan and Ignacio and a crowd of other children and grown people whose names I cannot tell you because I do not know them all.

As they passed the chapel, Doña Teresa came out and slipped into line behind the Twins. If she had been looking in the right direction just at that minute she might have seen two dark figures come out from behind some bushes near the priest's house, and though they had no candles, fall in at the end of the procession and march with them to the entrance of the Big House. But she kept her eyes on her candle, which she was afraid might be blown out by the wind.

When they reached the doorway every one stopped while Lupito and his new wife sang a song saying that the night was cold and dark and the wind was blowing, and asking for shelter, just as if they were Joseph and Mary, and the Big House were the inn in Bethlehem.

Then a voice came from the inside of the Big House as if it were the innkeeper himself answering Joseph and Mary. It was really the mozo's voice, and it said, No, they could not come in, that there was no more room in the inn.

Then Lupito and his wife sang again and told the innkeeper that she who begged admittance and had not where to lay her head, was indeed the Queen of Heaven.

At this name the door was flung wide open, and the priest, bearing the images of the Virgin and Child and Joseph, entered with Lupito and all the others singing behind him.

The priest led the procession through the entrance arch to the patio, and there he placed the images in a shrine, all banked with palms and flowering plants, which had been placed in the patio on purpose to receive them.

Then he lifted his hand and prayed, and blessed the people, and the whole procession passed in front of the images, each one kneeling before them long enough to leave his lighted candle stuck in a little framework before the shrine. Señor Fernandez and his wife Carmen watched the scene from one end of the patio.

Doña Teresa and the Twins were among the first ones to leave their candles, and afterward they stood under the gallery which ran around the patio, to watch the rest of the procession.

Everything was quiet until this was done, because this part of Christmas was just like a church service. One by one the people knelt before the images, crossed themselves, and joined the group under the gallery. Last of all came the two dark figures without any candles.

Up to that moment they had lingered behind the others in the background, and had kept as much as possible in the shadow, but now they stood right in front of the Holy Family with all the candles shining directly into their brown faces—and who should they be but Pancho and Pedro come back from the war?

II

The moment she saw Pancho, Doña Teresa gave a loud scream of joy, and then she rushed right by every one—almost stepping on the toes of the priest himself—and threw her arms around his neck, while the Twins, who got there almost as soon as she did, clasped an arm or a leg, or whatever part of their father they could get hold of.

At the same time Pedro's wife, with her baby on her arm and Pablo beside her, made a dash for Pedro, but Pablo got there first because, you remember, his mother was fat. And Pedro was so glad to see them he tried to hug her and the baby both at once, while Pablo hung round his neck, only as he was a small man he couldn't begin to reach round, and had to take them one at a time after all.

Everybody was so glad to see Pancho and Pedro, and so glad for the happiness that had come to their wives and children on Christmas Day that everybody shook hands with everybody else, and talked and asked questions without waiting for anybody to answer them, until it sounded almost like the animals on San Ramon's Day.

After Pancho and Pedro had greeted their families, and had said how Pablo and the Twins had grown, and Pedro's wife had told him that the baby had six teeth, and the baby had bitten Pedro's finger to prove it, he and Pancho broke away from them and went to pay their respects to Señor Fernandez and the priest, who were standing together, talking in low tones and watching the crowd round the wanderers.

Pancho and Pedro had reason to dread what Señor Fernandez and the priest might say to them. They thought the priest might say, "Is this obedience, my sons?" and they thought very possibly Señor Fernandez might say something like this: "Well, my men, do you think you can play fast and loose with your job like that? You'll have to learn a hacienda can't be run that way. There's plenty of other help, so you may see if you can find work elsewhere."

But as they came before Señor Fernandez and bowed humbly with their sombreros in their hands, the priest glanced at their ragged clothes and their thin faces and said something in a low tone to Señor Fernandez, and although Pancho and Pedro listened they couldn't hear a word of it except "Christmas Day."

Señor Fernandez gazed at them rather sternly for a moment without speaking and then he said: "Well, Pancho and Pedro, I suppose you've been out seeing the world, and would like to have your old jobs back again, eh? You don't deserve it, you rascals, but I think I can use the men who have taken your places elsewhere on the hacienda, so if you like you can take your boat again the first of the year, Pedro; and Pancho, you can begin your rounds next week. Now, go and enjoy yourselves with your families!"

And if you'll believe me, he never even asked them where they had been! Pancho and Pedro went back to their wives, who were watching the interview anxiously from the other side of the patio, and the wives knew the moment they saw the men's faces that everything was all right and they could be happy once more.

The rest of the people had already gone into the dining-room of the Big House and were eagerly watching a great earthenware boat that hung from the middle of the ceiling. They knew that the boat was full of good things to eat. Beside the boat stood pretty Carmen with a long stick in one hand and a white cloth in the other.

As Pancho and Pedro with their wives and Pedro's baby came into the room, she was saying: "Now, I'll blindfold each of you, one at a time, and you must whack the piñata real hard or nothing at all will happen! I'll begin!"

She tied the cloth about her own eyes, turned round three times, and then struck out with the stick. But she didn't come anywhere near the piñata. Instead she nearly cracked José's head!

Everybody laughed, and then it was Lupito's turn. Lupito was a great man at roping bulls, or breaking wild horses, but he couldn't hit the boat with his eyes covered any better than Carmen had.

Then José tried. He struck the piñata — but it was only a love-pat. The boat swung back and forth a little, but not a thing dropped overboard.

At last Carmen cried out, "Come, Tonio, see if you have not a better aim than the rest of us."

Tonio stepped boldly into the middle of the room and Carmen bandaged his eyes, turned him round and gave him the stick. Tonio knew what was in that boat, and he was bound to get it out if he could, so he struck out with a kind of sideways sweep and struck the ship whack on the prow!

It was made of earthenware on purpose so it would break easily, and the moment Tonio struck it there was a crashing sound, and then a perfect rain of cakes and candies, and bananas, and oranges, and peanuts, and other goodies which fell all over the floor, and it wasn't two minutes before every one in the room had his mouth full and both hands sticky.

Doña Teresa and Pancho watched the fun for a while, and then Doña Teresa whispered to Pancho: "My angel, when did you eat last? You look hungry."

Pancho at that very moment had his mouth full of banana, but he managed to say: "Last night I had some tortillas. I have had nothing since until now."

"Bless my soul!" cried Doña Teresa. "Come home with me at once. Thanks be to the Holy Virgin, you'll share the turkey with us after all! I had to cook him because we couldn't catch the rooster! Tell the Twins and come right along."

III

So while the guitars were tinkling and the rest of the people were still singing and dancing and having the merriest kind of a merry Christmas, Pancho and his family said good-night politely to Señor Fernandez and his wife and slipped quietly away to the little adobe hut under the fig tree.

When they were inside their little home once more, Doña Teresa made a fire in the brasero and heated some of the turkey for Pancho, and while he ate, Tonio and Tita stood on each side of their one chair, in which he sat, and listened with their eyes and mouths both while their father told about his adventures as a Soldier of the Revolution. And then they told him all about the night they were lost, and the secret meeting, and he was so astonished that he could hardly believe they had not dreamed it until Tita told him just what the Tall Man had said, and what Pedro had said, and about the pebble that rolled down.

Then he said, "Have you told any one about this?"

And Doña Teresa answered proudly, "Not a soul. Not even the priest."

"You've done well, then," Pancho said. "The Tall Man punishes those who spoil his plans by talking of them. He has raised an army of two thousand men in such ways. We enlisted for only four months, and in that time we turned the region to the south of us altogether into the hands of theRevolutionists. I intended to return home at the end of the four months, but finally stayed a month more to finish the campaign."

"I knew you would come some time, my angel," cried Doña Teresa. "I have prayed every day before the Virgin for your safe return."

"As God wills it," Pancho answered soberly. "I meant at any rate to strike my blow for freedom, and to try to make things better for us all."

"Well, have you?" asked Doña Teresa.

Pancho scratched his head with the old puzzled expression on his face. "I don't know," he said at last. "Things are not right as they are,—I know that,—and they never will be right if no one ever complains or protests or makes any fuss about it. And I know, too, that these uprisings never will stop until Mexico is better governed, and poor people have the chance they long for and do not know how to get for themselves. It is something just to keep things stirred up. Perhaps some time Tonio here can think out what ought to be done. He may even be a great general some day."

"Heaven forbid!" cried Doña Teresa. She almost upset Pancho's dish, she was so emphatic. "There has been enough of going to war in this family!"

"Well," said Pancho, "war isn't very pleasant. I've seen enough of it to know that: but peace isn't very pleasant either, when your life is without hope and you must live like the animals—if you live at all."

"Now that I have you at home again, I, for one, am quite content," said Doña Teresa; and then she went to unroll the mats and put the children to bed.

They were so tired that they went to sleep in their corner in no time at all, and when she had snuffed the candles before the Virgin, Doña Teresa came back to Pancho and sat with him beside the embers still glowing in the brasero.

She told him everything that had happened on the hacienda while he was away, and Pancho told her all the strange sights he had seen, and the new things he had learned, and at last he said:—

"Anyway, I've made up my mind that Tonio shall have more learning than he can get on this hacienda, though I don't know yet how it can be brought about. Somehow children must know more than their parents if things are ever to be better for the poor people of Mexico."

And Doña Teresa answered, "Well, anyway, we have each other and the Twins, so let's take comfort in that, right now, even if there are many things in the world that can't be set right yet awhile."

Just then the first streak of dawn showed red over the eastern hills. Out in the fig tree the red rooster shook himself and crowed, and to Pancho, as he stretched himself on his own hard bed in his own poor little home once more, it sounded exactly as if he said,

> "Cock-a-doodle-do-oo.
>
> We're glad to see you-oo-oo."